This Book Belongs to

For Mrs Finning and Form One – R.P.

With love to my wee boys!
Ruaraidh and Jamie – M.R.

First published in Great Britain in 2006 by Andersen Press Ltd., 20 Vauxhall Bridge Road, London SW1V 2SA.
This paperback edition first published in 2008 by Andersen Press Ltd.
Published in Australia by Random House Australia Pty., Level 3, 100 Pacific Highway, North Sydney, NSW 2060.
Text copyright © Rebecca Patterson, 2006. Illustration copyright © Mary Rees, 2006.
The rights of Rebecca Patterson and Mary Rees to be identified as the author and
illustrator of this work have been asserted by them in accordance with the
Copyright, Designs and Patents Act, 1988.
All rights reserved. Colour separated in Switzerland by Photolitho AG, Zürich.
Printed and bound in Singapore.

10   9   8   7   6   5   4   3   2   1

British Library Cataloguing in Publication Data available.

ISBN 978 1 84270 572 8

This book has been printed on acid-free paper

The *The* Gordon Star

by Rebecca Patterson
Illustrated by Mary Rees

ANDERSEN PRESS

One Monday morning Miss Conway was giving
Lucy a gold star for doing some neat handwriting.
"Well done, Lucy!" said Miss Conway.
"Another gold star!"

Gordon meanwhile was pulling his funniest face.
The children round him were laughing.
Miss Conway didn't laugh, she said,
"Settle down, Class One, it's time for Art."

She gave everyone a ball of clay and told them to make animals.

Peter's elephant was so good Miss Conway held it up
for everyone to admire.
Gordon was working hard, making a little bear, but
it wasn't coming out right, so he turned it into a duck.
But then the clay didn't look like anything at all!

Gordon rolled the clay back into a ball. All the other children had finished their animals and Miss Conway was collecting them onto a tray to dry.

When Miss Conway saw Gordon's clay ball she said,
"What's this?"
Gordon looked hard at his clay ball and said . . .

"I think it's a little dinosaur egg that hasn't hatched yet!"
Class One laughed and Gordon laughed too. Miss Conway smiled and sent the class out to play football.

Rachel was the best at football. She kicked the ball really hard and it zoomed towards the goal. It hit little Alan Cole on the head and he burst into tears.

Rachel kept saying sorry but Alan was still crying
and rubbing his head.
Gordon ran up, cheering and shouting,
"What a save!"

Alan stopped crying and Gordon chanted,
"Who's the best in the goal?
Let's all shout it! Alan Cole!"
Alan Cole was a hero.

Afterwards it was maths. Martha was almost crying because the sums were so hard. She didn't have enough fingers to add 8 + 9. Gordon whispered, "We'll have to use our toes as well!" He took off his shoes and socks. Martha laughed.

At the end of maths Miss Conway told Gordon to put his shoes and socks back on but she gave Martha a gold star for making good progress.

At lunch time, Gordon became Giant Gordon, the Enemy of Peas. Peas were running all over his plate and screaming. They tried to hide from him under the mashed potato. Giant Gordon growled as he caught and ate them.

After lunch Gordon had to stay behind to clear up his mess. Peas had escaped all over the floor.

In the afternoon it was time for the fun geography quiz. The class was in two teams but no one picked Gordon. "Come on, Class One," said Miss Conway. "Who wants Gordon on their team?"

It was very quiet. Someone whispered,
"No one, Gordon is rubbish at geography!"
And someone else whispered back,
"Yeah, Gordon is rubbish at everything!"

Miss Conway didn't hear, but Gordon did.
He looked at the star chart and his name with no stars
next to it and then he started to cry. Everyone was amazed
because Gordon never cried. Gordon never looked sad.

Then Gordon shouted, "I am rubbish!"
Class One gasped, Gordon had never been cross
before either.
"I am rubbish in art! I am rubbish at football!
I am rubbish at geography quiz and I am no good
at eating lunch! And I'll never get a gold star!"

Then Alan Cole, who still had a bump on his head, said, "But you are good at cheering us up!"

And Martha said, "And helping!"
And someone else shouted,
"Gordon's very funny!"
Suddenly everyone was calling out great things
about Gordon.

Miss Conway told them to calm down.
She thought for a moment and said,
"Class One, you are right. Gordon is kind,
cheerful, helpful and very funny!"

And she gave Gordon his first gold star. Then she said, "Every day, from now on, I will give a gold star to someone for being just like Gordon: helpful, cheerful, funny and kind. We will call it . . .

. . . the Gordon Star."

Other picture books you might enjoy:

9781842706114

NICKy

Tony and Zoë Ross

9781842705735

The Opposite

Tom MacRae
Elena Odriozola

9781842704691

Once Upon An Ordinary School Day

Colin McNaughton   Satoshi Kitamura